Santa Will Come Tonight

by Dawn Apperley

Cartwheel
·B·O·O·K·S·

SCHOLASTIC INC.

New York   Toronto   London   Auckland   Sydney
Mexico City   New Delhi   Hong Kong   Buenos Aires

Snow is falling in the forest.
Christmas day is almost here.
Santa Claus will come tonight.
He brings presents every year.

Santa Claus will come tonight
When we're asleep
and tucked in tight.

Whizzing round the pond,
Slipping on the ice,
Little chipmunks, showing off,
Spin round once, spin round twice.

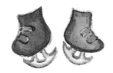

Santa Claus will come tonight
When we're asleep
and tucked in tight.

Among the frosty snowmen,
  Rolling balls of snow,
The squirrels, planning mischief,
  Pack the snow and . . . throw!

Santa Claus will come tonight
When we're asleep
  and tucked in tight.

Way up high on snowy slopes,
Ready, steady: one, two, three,
Little deer go down, down, down
And sleigh way past the Christmas tree.

Santa Claus will come tonight
When we're asleep
and tucked in tight.

Aloft among the branches,
Cardinals deck the trees
With pretty bows and bells
That jingle in the breeze.

Santa Claus will come tonight
When we're asleep
and tucked in tight.

Standing in the starlight,
  Beneath a crescent moon,
Mice sing Christmas carols. . . .
  Guess who's coming soon?

Santa Claus will come tonight
  When we're asleep
    and tucked in tight.

Cutting Christmas cookies,
Helping Mama bake,
Little foxes try some:
    "Don't get a tummy ache!"

Santa Claus will come tonight
When we're asleep
    and tucked in tight.

Their stockings by the fire—
   Blue, green, purple, yellow, red—
Little bunnies kiss their papa,
   Then they hop right into bed.

Santa Claus will come tonight
When we're asleep
   and tucked in tight.

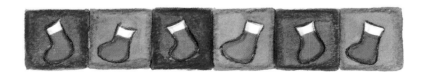

Flying through the sky,
   With gifts for large and small,
Eight reindeer and a jolly elf
   Wish peace and love to all.

   Santa Claus is here tonight
      While we're asleep
         and tucked in tight.

ISBN 0-439-40449-5

Copyright © 2002 by Dawn Apperley.
All rights reserved. Published by Scholastic Inc.
SCHOLASTIC, CARTWHEEL BOOKS, and associated logos are trademarks
and/or registered trademarks of Scholastic Inc.

10 9 8 7 6 5 4 3 2 1   02 03 04 05 06

Printed in China   62
First Scholastic printing, October 2002